Hanuman to the Rescue

Born in 1934, Ruskin Bond grew up in Jamnagar, Shimla, New Delhi and Dehradun. He has been writing for over sixty years and now has over 120 titles in print—novels, collections of stories, poetry, essays, anthologies and books for children. His first novel, *The Room on the Roof*, received the prestigious John Llewellyn Rhys Prize in 1957. He has also received the Padma Shri, and two awards from the Sahitya Akademi—one for his short stories and another for his writings for children. In 2012, the Delhi government gave him its Lifetime Achievement Award. He lives in Mussoorie with his adopted family.

Prasun Mazumdar is an illustrator, painter and graphic designer. He studied at the National Institute of Fashion Technology, Delhi, from where he received a Bachelor's degree in design. Prasun has illustrated and designed children's books such as *The Kashmiri Storyteller* and *Secrets*, both by Ruskin Bond, and *Gind* by Harini Gopalswami Srinivasan.

Hanuman to the Rescue

RUSKIN BOND

Illustrated by
Prasun Mazumdar

RED TURTLE
RUPA

Published in
RED TURTLE by Rupa Publications India Pvt. Ltd 2013
7/16, Ansari Road, Daryaganj
New Delhi 110002

Sales Centres:
Bengaluru Chennai
Hyderabad Jaipur Kathmandu
Kolkata Mumbai Prayagraj

Text copyright © Ruskin Bond 1993, 2013
Illustration copyright © Rupa Publications India Pvt. Ltd 2013

This is a work of fiction. Names, characters, places and incidents are either the product of the author's imagination or are used fictitiously, and any resemblance to any actual persons, living or dead, events or locales is entirely coincidental.

All rights reserved.
No part of this publication may be reproduced, transmitted, or stored in a retrieval system, in any form or by any means, electronic, mechanical, photocopying, recording or otherwise, without the prior permission of the publisher.

ISBN: 978-81-291-2462-3

Fifth impression 2025

10 9 8 7 6 5

The moral right of the author has been asserted.

Printed in India

This book is sold subject to the condition that it shall not, by way of trade or otherwise, be lent, resold, hired out, or otherwise circulated, without the publisher's prior consent, in any form of binding or cover other than that in which it is published.

Introduction

This retelling of the adventures of Rama and Sita was originally written by me for very young readers in the UK, and I tried to tell the story in a simple, unadorned style, knowing that most British children would be unfamiliar with Hindu religion and mythology.

The storybook was called *The Adventures of Rama and Sita*, and was first published by Julia MacRae Books, London, in 1987.

The text of this edition is exactly the same, only the title has been changed. My grandson, Gautam, was particularly fond of Hanuman, and wanted him in the title. One can't disappoint a grandson. Hence the change in title.

Ruskin Bond

The Banishment of Rama

All through the warm summer night, the people of Ayodhya worked to prepare their city for the morrow's celebrations, the coronation of their beloved prince, Rama. They hung gay lanterns from balconies and treetops, and adorned the white temples of the city with banners and bamboo archways. They burned fragrant incense and strewed flowers on all sides—roses, jasmine, marigolds. The people were in great good humour; there was not one who did not look forward to the celebrations, for Rama and his young wife, Sita, were the idols of the people's hearts.

Now, although Rama was to be crowned, his father, King Dasaratha, was still alive. But the old king felt too tired and weak to perform his royal duties unaided. And so, from his four sons, Rama, Bharat, Lakshman and Shatrughan, he had chosen

Rama, his firstborn, to share the throne with him.

Unfortunately for Rama, he had two dangerous enemies in the palace, through no fault of his own. They were Queen Kaikeyi, his stepmother, and her old maidservant Manthara, who was devoted to her mistress and knew all her secrets. On this night of joyous preparation, the two women were standing at a window in the palace, looking gloomily at the crowded streets below.

'Oh, Manthara,' Queen Kaikeyi said bitterly, 'if only these preparations were for my own son, Bharat, instead of for Rama, the king's favourite.'

'And why shouldn't they be?' said Manthara. 'Isn't Prince Bharat also beloved of his father, the king?'

'What do you mean?' asked the Queen impatiently. 'Do you think the King would place Bharat before Rama at *my* request?'

'Stranger things than that have happened,' said Manthara. And she reminded Kaikeyi how, years ago, the Queen had saved King Dasaratha's life by tending his wounds upon a battlefield, and how, in return, the grateful king had sworn to grant her two favours, at any time that she should ask for them.

'You have never claimed your rights,' continued Manthara, 'but the time has come for those favours to be granted. Listen, my queen.'

And drawing nearer her mistress, she whispered a few words into her ear that made the queen's eyes light up with excitement.

'Oh, wise Manthara,' she cried. 'I will do as you say.' And as dawn was now at hand, there was no time to be lost as the

celebrations would begin soon after sunrise, Kaikeyi hurried to the king's apartment.

'My lord,' she said eagerly to the old king who was reclining upon his couch, 'tell me this! Do you remember how I saved your life upon the battlefield long ago?'

'How could I forget your loving skill?' answered the king. 'Nor have I forgotten the promise that I made you at that time. Have you come to ask for your two favours now, my Kaikeyi?'

The queen bowed her head in assent.

'Ask those boons of me now,' said the unsuspecting king, 'and I swear by my dear son Rama, that if it is in my power to grant your requests, they will be granted.'

'Then,' said Kaikeyi in triumph, 'grant me two things, oh King. Let our son Bharat be crowned this day, and let Rama be banished to the forest of Dandak for fourteen years.'

The king nearly swooned with dismay and anger.

'What are you saying?' he cried, his voice

shaking. 'How can you be so treacherous! What wrong has Rama ever done you? No, such requests shall not be granted.'

'As you like,' replied Kaikeyi calmly. 'But you realize, of course, that your subjects will come to know of your broken promises to me. You will for ever be known throughout the land as the king who failed to keep his solemn vow. You will always be spoken of with scorn.'

Dasartha knew that he was in the queen's power, for a king always had to be true to his word and had he not vowed, in the name of his dear son, that he would grant her requests, cruel though they had proved to be? In vain, he begged the queen to ask him any other favour, but she had set her mind on Rama's banishment. She thought that if Rama were sent to Dandak, a forest said to be full of demons and evil spirits, it was most unlikely that he would return alive after the years of exile.

Finding he could do nothing to make the queen change her mind, Dasaratha resigned himself to his fate, and with an aching heart, he entered the great audience chamber in the palace, where eager crowds were awaiting him.

To the amazement of everyone in the hall, the king announced that Bharat, not Rama, was to share his throne. There were cries of surprise and dismay from the people, and Prince Rama, puzzled and unhappy, stepped forward. The excited crowd began to cheer him as he stood before the throne.

'What have I done, my father?' he asked with simple dignity. 'Why have you dishonoured me?'

The king could no longer control his grief. With many bitter tears he spoke of his vow to Kaikeyi—how her demands had to be granted, cruel and unjust though they might be.

'Not only must I deprive you of the throne,' said the king despairingly, 'but it is the desire of the queen that you be banished to the forest of Dandak for fourteen years.'

When Bharat realized what had happened, he took Rama's hand and vowed that he would never take the throne from his brother.

But Rama, who had listened to his father's words in silence, now said, 'No, Bharat, the crown is yours. I must honour my father's promise. I will go to the forest of Dandak, and not until fourteen years have passed will I return to Ayodhya.'

'You will not go alone,' rang out a young woman's voice, and the beautiful, dark-eyed Sita, who until that moment had been overcome by grief and fear at the strange turn of events, now came and stood by her husband's side.

'I must share your exile,' she said. 'Alone here, I would surely die.'

'But the forest of Dandak is full of danger,' said Rama gently. 'You know well that Ravana, the king of the demons, is said to haunt it with his wicked followers. They are always looking for an opportunity to work their evil upon the good and innocent.'

'And I must accompany you too, Rama,' said Prince Lakshman, the king's second son, who had always been devoted to Rama. 'I will help you protect Sita.'

Rama protested that he could not allow his wife and brother to endure the hardship of forest life, but Sita and Lakshman begged to be allowed to

accompany him. At last, he gave way to them. Then he turned to the king, and embracing the old man tenderly, he said, 'Farewell, father. I do not blame you, for you have been the victim of the queen's cunning.'

So, amidst great sorrowing, Rama, Sita and Lakshman took leave of all those who loved them in the palace, and, after changing their royal robes for the plain clothes of forest folk, they set out towards the deep, dark woods of Dandak which lay to the south of the kingdom.

In the Forest of Dandak

Scarcely had the three exiles left the palace, than King Dasaratha fell into a coma from which his physicians could not revive him, and a few days later he was dead.

'Now,' thought Kaikeyi, 'Bharat will be crowned at last.'

But the Queen was doomed to disappointment, for Bharat refused to ascend the throne, saying that Rama must be brought back from the forest to take his rightful place as King. Kaikeyi begged her son not to throw away his chance at glory, but Bharat was determined to see justice done, so he journeyed to the forest of Dandak and managed to overtake Rama and his companions.

Rama was deeply grieved to hear of his father's death, but he refused to listen to Bharat's pleas that he return to be crowned the king of Ayodhya.

'My father pledged his word that I should remain in exile for fourteen years,' he said firmly, 'and I will remain here in fulfilment of his vow.'

'Then I will govern the people as your regent,' said Bharat, 'until the day you return.'

So Bharat took leave of the wanderers and, returning to Ayodhya, he governed the kingdom with wisdom and justice, but, true to his word, refused to be crowned. He set a pair of Rama's slippers upon the throne as a sign of his absent brother's authority.

Kaikeyi had failed to make her son the real king, but neither she nor Manthara gave up hope, for they felt sure that Rama would never return from the forest of Dandak.

Meanwhile, the wanderers went deeper into the forest, living upon fruits and herbs. Sometimes they came across a tiny hermitage in which lived some holy man who gave them hospitality. Otherwise they did not see a living soul in the forest. And although they were always on their guard against the demon King Ravana and his followers, so far not a single evil spirit had appeared or troubled them.

One day, they chanced to arrive at a little hermitage which was inhabited by an old priest of great repute named Agastya.

The holy man welcomed them, and was astonished to hear that they had been in the forest for so long without being attacked by demons.

'Since I am a hermit, Ravana and his followers do not bother to molest me,' he said. 'But I have often seen them lurking near this place, and I fear that you may be attacked by them. It is possible that you have been destined by the Gods to wage war upon these evil spirits who trouble the earth so much. I will give you my store of weapons.'

Then, to Rama's delight, Agastya presented him with a bow and a quiver full of an endless store of arrows. Lakshman received a golden-sheathed sword.

'These weapons once belonged to the great

god Indra,' said Agastya. 'Their aim is true and deadly. Now you may wander where you will, for the demons are afraid of these arrows and this sword.'

As Rama touched his bow with loving fingers, he solemnly vowed to himself that he would rid the world of all evil.

They rested for a while at the hermitage, then Rama said, 'Oh, best and wisest among the sages, please direct us to some pleasant place, where we may spend the remaining years of our exile.'

'Seek the vale of Panchavati,' advised Agastya. 'It is a pleasant, fertile glade where you may live in comfort and peace.'

So the wanderers took leave of him and continued on their journey, armed with the precious weapons.

Following the sage's directions, they soon reached the vale of Panchavati, which was indeed a beautiful, tranquil spot. There, magnolia blossomed and the mango trees were laden with fruit. Peacocks danced in the forest clearings, and many-hued parrots flew swiftly from tree to tree. A little stream of fresh water wound its way through the glade.

'Let us remain here,' cried Sita eagerly, so the brothers set to work to build her a small dwelling.

This was soon done, and Sita was as delighted with her new home as if it had been a palace. The walls of the hut were made of hardened earth instead of marble, and in the place of gleaming columns, pillars of bamboo supported the thatched roof. But they were happy in this simple abode, and as the years slipped peacefully by, Rama felt convinced that the demons would never trouble them. Had not Agastya given them protection with his magic weapons?

But he was soon to discover his mistake, and to learn from bitter experience that magic weapons alone were not enough to protect the good and innocent from the evil designs of King Ravana.

The Demon King

Ravana, the king of the demons, was determined to do something about the royal forest dwellers, as he was the sworn enemy of gods and virtuous mortals. He knew that the sage Agastya had given them magic weapons,

and realized that it would be dangerous for him to attack the brothers openly. He had to find some way of slaying them by stealth. So he constantly lurked unseen near the vale of Panchavati, in the hope of meeting the brothers unarmed; but as yet he had not seen them without their weapons.

However, one evening while Ravana was watching them from a distance, he had an idea which made him very pleased with himself.

'Sita is most beautiful,' he said to himself, 'and she is dearer to Rama than his very life. No longer will I waste time trying to kill the proud prince. Instead I will steal from him his most cherished possession. Sita shall be mine!'

The longer Ravana thought about his scheme, the more it delighted him, although he knew that the capture of Sita would be no easy task, for neither Rama nor Lakshman ever left her unguarded for a moment. Still, Ravana had all the aids of sorcery at his command, and he decided to ask the help of his brother, Marichi, who was said to be the most cunning of all the demon race.

Marichi lived alone in a distant part of the forest,

so Ravana sent for his chariot.

The chariot was a golden vehicle drawn by two fierce-looking asses with goblins heads. Not only could this strange car roll over the ground with great swiftness, but it could also fly through the air like an aeroplane. Ravana stepped inside his car and flew to the most gloomy part of the forest, where Marichi was studying the arts of magic.

'Greetings, brother!' cried Ravana. 'I have come to you for help. You know that Rama, Prince of Ayodhya, has dared to enter this forest with Sita, his wife, and his brother, Lakshman?'

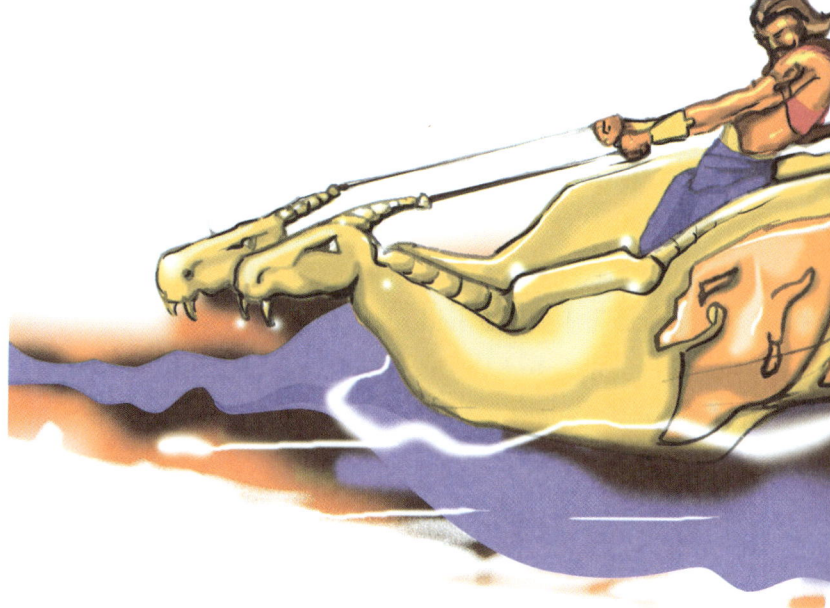

Hanuman to the Rescue

'Yes, Ravana,' said Marichi gloomily. 'But take care. Do not molest those mortals, for I have a strong feeling that they will bring trouble upon us.'

Ravana laughed at his brother's words, but Marichi remained serious.

'I think the gods themselves have sent this powerful prince to destroy us,' he said. 'Did you know, brother, that the magic arrows of Agastya are in his possession?'

'Yes, I know,' answered Ravana, 'and that is why I do not plan to fight him. But listen! What I propose

to do will injure him more than death.'

Then Ravana told his brother how he planned to carry Sita away to his enchanted palace on the distant island of Lanka.

'She shall become my queen,' he said. 'And Rama will look for her in vain, for no mortal can cross the seas which divide Lanka from this land.'

'You shall get no help from me, brother,' said Marichi firmly, 'for I know that disaster will be in store for us if we do anything to harm Rama. Let Sita be, I beg you. Go back and find another, more beautiful bride.'

But Ravana was not to be put off by his brother, and as he knew that he would never be able to carry out his scheme without Marichi's aid, he raised his sword and shouted, 'Refuse to help me, and you shall die instantly!'

Seeing that Ravana was in deadly earnest, Marichi gave in, saying, 'It is better for me to be killed by Rama than by you. At least then I would lose my life to an enemy.'

Ravana was overjoyed and embraced his brother, saying, 'Now you are again my dear old Marichi!'

And stepping inside the chariot, they set out for the vale of Panchavati.

The Golden Deer

Rama and his companions were enjoying the cool dawn of a summer's morning, before the sun rose in fiery splendour and forced them to seek shelter. Lakshman wandered a little way from the glade in search of fresh fruits, while Rama and Sita busied themselves with household tasks.

'Oh, look!' cried Sita suddenly, pointing to a young gazelle which had just bounded into sight. 'Such a beautiful little creature! How graceful it is and how lovely its shining coat. Like living gold! I wish it were mine.'

'And what would you do with it?' asked Rama.

'I would make it my play fellow,' she answered wistfully. 'And when the long years of our exile have passed, I would take it with me to Ayodhya.'

'You shall have your desire,' said Rama, and he darted in pursuit of the gazelle, but the timid little creature sprang back and hid itself among the trees.

Sita gave a cry of disappointment, and the gazelle reappeared, only to elude Rama's grasp once more by springing still further into the forest.

'I will catch the animal for you, never fear,' said Rama, and called out to his brother, 'Lakshman, come and look after Sita while I catch this deer.'

Lakshman returned to the glade to remain with Sita, and Rama, picking up his bow and arrows, ran swiftly after the gazelle, which was darting about in a tantalizing fashion. First, it led Rama through some thickets, then it rushed far into the forest. It went so far that the prince grew hot and weary. But he would not give up the pursuit.

'This is the first thing Sita has asked for since we came to live in the forest,' he told himself. 'If it is in my power to grant it, she shall have her wish.'

On bounded the gazelle, now coming near Rama, now hiding itself, until at last, when the prince realized how far he had travelled from the vale of Panchavati, he began to feel uneasy.

'This is not the way of an innocent wild creature,' he thought. 'What if this is some trick of the demons to lure me away from Sita! It's a good thing Lakshman is with her.' Once more the gazelle darted towards him, then, as Rama raised his hand, it sprang away.

'No,' said the puzzled Prince, 'even if I were to capture this animal, it would not be a fit playmate for Sita. Instead, I will kill the creature and take her its golden fur.'

So Rama drew his bow and let fly one of his magic arrows. Immediately, the animal fell to the ground and Rama felt a pang of remorse for having injured such a beautiful creature.

And then a strange thing happened.

The gazelle began to change its shape until it took the form of a demon with a deadly wound in his side!

It was Marichi who, by means of his sorcery, had

turned himself into a gazelle, hoping to lure both Rama and Lakshman from Sita's side.

Half the demon's work had been done, for here was Rama, far from his wife but, as he looked upon the Prince with eyes of hatred, Marichi made one last effort to complete the task that Ravana had set him.

'Help, Lakshman, help!' he shouted in a voice which was exactly like Rama's. Then the demon fell back lifeless, whilst Rama stood by with wonder and disquiet in his heart.

Marichi's dying cry had echoed through the forest, as far as the vale of Panchavati, and at the terrible sound, Sita looked at Lakshman in terror.

Hanuman to the Rescue

'It was the voice of Rama!' she cried. 'He is in danger. Go quickly to him, Lakshman!'

'No, Sita,' said Lakshman gravely. 'I cannot leave you, for I gave my word to Rama that I would remain with you during his absence.'

'Oh, do go, I implore you,' cried Sita, almost in tears. 'Hurry, brother, or you will be too late.'

'Calm yourself,' said Lakshman. 'It was the voice of some evil spirit in the forest. Why should Rama call for help? He can protect himself with the magic arrows of Agastya.'

But Sita refused to be comforted. 'Are you a coward?' she cried bitterly. 'Are you afraid to help your brother?'

She continued to taunt him until, at last, Lakshman agreed to go. Begging her not to leave the hut no matter what happened, he hurried away in the direction from which the mysterious cry had come.

The Capture of Sita

Sita was not afraid of being left alone, but she could not bear the thought that Lakshman might arrive too late to help Rama. She blamed herself for the foolish whim that had sent Rama off in the quest of the gazelle.

The moments passed, and each one seemed like an hour to Sita as she crouched by the hut, watching every movement of the trees and listening intently for the sound of footsteps. Presently, she heard a rustling in the bushes and she sprang to her feet. A man stood there, but he was neither Rama nor Lakshman, only an old hermit with bowed shoulders and a flowing white beard.

As the old man drew near, Sita noticed with a pang of fear that a change had stolen over the forest. Until then, the sun had shone and the trees had been noisy with birdsong. Now there was nothing to be heard. Not a leaf rustled. The sky was suddenly overcast.

'May I rest here for a while?' asked the stranger in a feeble voice. 'I am tired and hungry.'

'I will bring you food and water,' said Sita timidly, and the old man thanked her. His gaze was steady, his eyes curiously bright and piercing.

'Who are you, lady?' he asked. 'And why do you live in this dangerous and lonely forest? Your beauty and grace should adorn a palace, not this rude hut.'

Sita told him how she had chosen to share the exile of her husband, and when she explained that her fancy for the gazelle had caused both Rama and Lakshman to leave her alone, the old man smiled to himself. Then he stood upright, and at once a change took place in him—his shrunken height increased to a mighty stature, his aged face grew youthful, bold and mocking, and his hermit's robe fell to the ground, revealing the regal clothes beneath. It was none other than the king of the demons who stood there—terrible Ravana himself!

Sita drew back with a cry of terror.

'Have no fear, Sita, I will not harm you,' said Ravana in a friendly manner. 'You must know that I am Ravana, the demon king, and I have come here to make you my queen. You will live in my beautiful palace on the island of Lanka and your days will be full of delight.'

He held out his arms, but Sita shrank from him, crying proudly: 'Don't you know that I am the wife of Prince Rama!'

'Rama will never return to you,' said Ravana. 'My brother Marichi has dealt with him. It was Marichi himself who took the form of a gazelle in order to lure Rama deep into the forest.'

Sita did not know whether to believe him or not, but on his face she saw nothing but triumph.

'You will come with me,' he ordered. His magic chariot appeared, and he forced her into it. As the chariot soared upwards, Sita felt that all was lost.

'You can carry me away,' she cried desperately, 'but I will never become your queen. I will remain faithful to Rama, whether he is alive or dead.'

Hanuman to the Rescue

Ravana's only reply was to urge his steeds to travel faster, for he saw in the distance a dark speck coming towards him, and he was afraid that someone was already in pursuit.

Nearer came this strange speck and Ravana recognized it as Jatayu, the king of the vultures, who had always been an enemy of the demon race.

'Stop, Ravana!' cried the great bird as he soared above the chariot. 'Where are you taking her?'

'Oh good bird, help me!' called Sita. 'I am the wife of Prince Rama, and this cruel king has captured me by cunning and force.'

'Let her go,' commanded Jatayu.

'Out of my way, ugly bird,' said Ravana scornfully.

Jatayu hurled herself fiercely upon Ravana but the demon king thrust his spear deep into the vulture's side.

'Sita, I cannot help you now,' moaned the wounded bird. 'May the gods protect you.' And gasping with pain, noble Jatayu sank down to the earth far below.

Ravana laughed in triumph and the chariot floated on, above plains and hills, and over a great mountain. Sita caught a glimpse of some huge monkeys moving about on the mountain. Acting on a sudden impulse, she loosened her scarf and necklace and let them fall into the hands of the creatures beneath her.

Onward flew the chariot, over villages and cities, until at last it neared the sea coast. Then away it flew over the stormy ocean, to the emerald isle of Lanka, where Sita was destined to spend several sad and lonely years.

After the strange death of the demon, Marichi,

Hanuman to the Rescue

Rama hurried back to the vale of Panchavati, but he had not gone far before he met Lakshman coming towards him.

'Where is Sita?' shouted Rama. 'You have left her unguarded!'

Lakshman began to explain what had happened but Rama cried out: 'Oh Lakshman, we have been tricked! Come quickly, for there is evil about in the forest.'

They rushed back, calling for Sita, but when they reached the hut they found it empty.

'The demons have stolen her,' said Rama and though the brothers continued to search for her, they could find no trace of her until they discovered the vulture, Jatayu, bleeding to death from the wound in his side.

'Are you searching for Sita, the wife of Rama?' asked the bird, raising his head with an effort.

'I received this wound in her defence. Ravana took her in his chariot...'

'Where—tell us where!' pleaded Rama. 'In which direction did they go?'

'Southwards,' whispered the dying bird. 'Towards

the highest mountain—take help from Sugriv, the Vanar King...' And then the great bird died.

In order to show their gratitude and respect for Jatayu, Rama and Lakshman lit a fire and gave the noble bird an honourable funeral. Then, with hope still alive in their hearts, they set out to find the mountain that lay to the south.

Hanuman to the Rescue

For many days their way lay through dark forest, but at last they reached open country once more, and beyond the wide plain which stretched before them, they could see a lofty mountain in the distance.

They hurried towards it, but just as they were about to start climbing, a huge monkey appeared from a dense thicket to bar their way.

'Stay where you are,' said the great animal fiercely. 'I am Hanuman, the minister of King Sugriv, who lives upon this mountain. Tell me why you are here.'

In spite of his fierce appearance and rough manner, there was something kindly in Hanuman's face, Rama felt.

To his joy he soon learned that not only had Hanuman seen Ravana's chariot flying southward, but that a woman in the car had flung down her ornaments, which happened to have fallen into Hanuman's hands. He showed Rama these treasures, and the Prince at once recognized Sita's silken scarf and glittering necklace.

'Perhaps our king can help you,' said Hanuman. 'Come, follow me to my master.'

As the big monkey led Rama and Lakshman up the mountain, he told them that Sugriv was really the king of the great monkey tribe called Vanars,

but that his wicked brother, Bali, had driven him from the kingdom and taken the throne for himself.

Sugriv had fled to this mountain, where he had lived in exile for some years, deserted by all his subjects except a few faithful warriors, of whom Hanuman was the chief.

'If you can help Sugriv to recover his throne,' said Hanuman, 'then he would gladly raise an army to attack Ravana, for the demons have always been enemies of our race.'

At the top of the mountain sat the exiled monkey king, brooding fiercely over his wrongs.

He was pleased to see Rama and Lakshman. Troubled by the demons as well as by his treacherous brother, he was glad to have the princes as his allies.

'If you possess mighty weapons, Prince,' he said, 'I beg you to help me, for I cannot deal with my cunning brother Bali on my own.'

Rama suggested that no time be lost, so he and Lakshman, in the company of their Vanar friends, journeyed to Sugriv's former kingdom.

When Bali heard that his brother was advancing

against him, he rushed forward to meet him, and they fell upon each other with cries of hatred and revenge. At first Rama stood by, hoping that Sugriv would win unaided, but Bali began to get the upper hand. In order to save Sugriv from a deadly blow, Rama let fly one of his magic arrows, which struck Bali dead. Sugriv was restored to his throne.

True to his word, King Sugriv sent four mighty armies north, south, east and west in order to discover where Ravana had hidden Sita. The southern army was commanded by Hanuman, who had vowed not to return without news of Sita.

He led his forces further and further south, through swamp and jungle, over hill and plain, to within sight of the ocean which washed the shores of the land. At last, he was rewarded for his tireless search.

At the top of a mountain, he found an old vulture called Sampati, the brother of the good Jatayu who had lost his life in the defence of Sita. Sampati had singed his wings in a bold attempt to fly over the sun, and he was now resting to recover from his injuries. He told Hanuman that, before he had fallen from the dizzy heights to which he had ascended, he had seen the chariot of Ravana coming down on the shores of the island of Lanka.

'There was someone struggling in the chariot,' said Sampati. 'She must have been Sita. But how will you rescue her? The island is surrounded by dangerous sea which only Ravana and his demons have been able to cross.'

Hanuman decided to visit Lanka by himself in order to discover how strong the demons were and what would be the best way of rescuing Sita. So, leaving his army to rest, he slipped away to the sea coast, but there he found that Sampati's warning was only too true. Stormy seas divided the island from the mainland.

But Hanuman did not give up easily. He had always been famed for his great prowess in leaping, and he decided to make an attempt to spring over the raging waters.

Hanuman to the Rescue

He climbed to the top of a rock, took one flying leap, and found himself on the shores of Lanka.

Hanuman's Tail of Fire

Hanuman looked about him, and was astonished that the place was so beautiful. The soft grass at his feet was studded with flowers, the trees around him were covered with spring blossoms. In the distance shone the white walls of a great city.

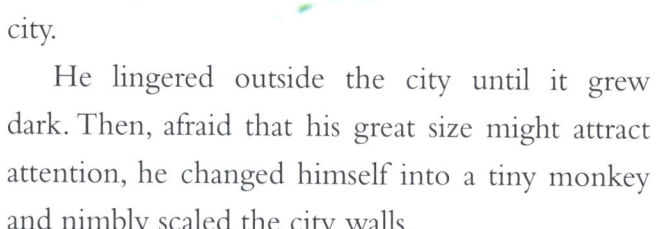

He lingered outside the city until it grew dark. Then, afraid that his great size might attract attention, he changed himself into a tiny monkey and nimbly scaled the city walls.

It did not take him long to find Ravana's palace.

He went from window to window but he could not see Sita in any of the apartments. For, having refused time and again to marry Ravana, she had been kept prisoner in a solitary part of the prison grounds, where she was guarded by several cruel demons who missed no opportunity to tease and torment her. Then, wandering in the palace gardens, Hanuman glimpsed a small white pavilion, half hidden in a grove of Asoka trees. He peeped through a window, and could hardly hold back a cry of joy, for there lay the most beautiful woman he had ever seen, and he knew that Sita was found at last. Her sorrow had made her pale and thin, but her goodness and beauty could not be destroyed.

He waited until she came to the window, and then in a gentle voice he whispered, 'Rama.'

Sita gave a start, but seeing no one except a tiny monkey before her, she thought she must have dreamt that she had heard Rama's name being whispered.

'Rama,' whispered Hanuman again, and this time he held out a golden ring which Rama had given him, and upon which the name of the prince was engraved.

At the sight of this token from her husband, Sita got very excited, but Hanuman begged her to control herself, for, should her demon guards discover him, his plans for her rescue might fail. But the guards paid no attention to the little chattering monkey, and he told Sita that he would bring Rama to her rescue without delay.

Already, he told her, an army was preparing to march on Lanka.

Unfortunately, as he was leaving the city, he could not resist the temptation of troubling Ravana. Changing back to his natural size, he tore up huge trees and stones and hurled them at the walls of Ravana's palace. He was enjoying himself so much that he failed to notice that demons were rushing to attack him from all directions. When at last he become aware of the danger, he seized a marble pillar as a weapon and leaped upon the roof of Ravana's palace.

'Long live Rama!' he cried, laying about with his marble club. 'I am Hanuman, friend of Rama, here to bring ruin upon Ravana and his demons!'

He took another leap, hoping that it would land him beyond

the reach of his enemies, but he was struck by an arrow and fell to the earth, surrounded by hordes of shrieking, revengeful demons.

Though Hanuman was only slightly wounded, he was now completely in the power of his enemies. They put him in chains and dragged him before Ravana.

'A quick death would be too small a punishment for this intruder,' declared Ravana. 'Set the spying ape alight, and let him slowly burn to death.'

The demons brought strips of cotton soaked in oil and bound them round Hanuman's tail; then they set fire to these rags and stood by to gloat over him.

When Sita was told what was happening, she offered a prayer to the God of fire: 'Oh, Agni! If there be any goodness in me, be good to Hanuman. Do not hurt him.'

The rags soaked in oil burned brightly, but the fire did not hurt Hanuman. He tore off his bonds with a mighty effort and leaped away from his astonished enemies, lashing his tail to and fro and setting fire to everything it touched. He jumped from one tall building to another, setting fire to them. In a little while, a strong breeze began to blow and half the city was in flames.

Hanuman went to the sea and, plunging in, put out the fire on his tail.

Then he rushed back to the pavilion to warn Sita to keep far away from the flames. Returning to the seashore, he crossed the ocean with another powerful leap and went in search of Rama.

The Battle Begins

Rama was overjoyed when he heard that Sita was alive and well. King Sugriv was quite willing to give him a huge army, and the Vanars came forward in thousands, thrilled at the chance of attacking their old enemies, the demons. But when these mighty forces, led by

Hanuman to the Rescue

Rama, Lakshman and Hanuman, reached the southern coast, they found that the ocean was still raging and it seemed impossible for the army to cross over to Lanka. Only Hanuman was capable of leaping over the waters.

'A bridge must be built for our forces,' said Rama. 'Let the most powerful Vanars throw great rocks and tree trunks into the ocean and you will see that in this way a causeway will be made for our army.'

Thousands of great Vanars immediately set to work. They uprooted trees and tore great rocks from the cliffs. When they were thrown into the sea, a bridge began to form that reached as far as the shores of Lanka in five days' time.

Then, during the night, Rama led the Vanar forces over the causeway and they landed in safety at Lanka, where they encamped some distance from the city.

Ravana had seen the approach of the enemy from a watch tower in his palace. When he saw the strength of the Vanar forces, he was filled with dismay. Rousing his men, he ordered them to make ready for battle without delay, and at daybreak, the demon king marched out of the city with thousands of fierce demon warriors.

Rama's forces were armed with great stones and uprooted tree trunks, which they hurled with all their might at the enemy, but, although countless demons were killed in this way, it seemed as if their ranks were never thinned. The brave Vanars suffered much from the poisoned spears and arrows which the demons used. At the end of the

Hanuman to the Rescue

first day's fighting, Lakshman was badly wounded. But Hanuman was at hand to apply healing herbs to the Prince's wounds, and Lakshman was soon able to take part in the battle again.

For many days and nights the fighting continued, and at first it seemed as if Ravana and his demons would triumph, but gradually, the tide of fortune began to turn in favour of Rama. One by one, Ravana's most powerful warriors fell before the magic arrows of Rama. In desperation, the demon king decided to force Kumbhakarn, his giant brother, to enter the fray.

Ravana Defeated

Hanuman to the Rescue

Now Kumbhakarn was the strongest of all the demons, an enormous giant of a demon. Unfortunately, he had always been a great source of trouble to Ravana, because when he moved, his huge clumsy limbs were apt to damage buildings and gardens. His appetite was so enormous that it could never be satisfied. As a result, Ravana had forced the poor giant to pass his days in slumber, and only twice a year was he allowed to wake up and enjoy a few hours' freedom.

It was not the right season for Kumbhakarn to be awakened, but Ravana gave orders that the giant be roused instantly and told of the desperate plight of the demon armies.

Waking Kumbhakarn, however, was a hard task, for though the demons clapped their hands and shouted, he did not move; nor did his peaceful snoring cease when trumpets were sounded in his ears. Elephants and camels were then brought into the giant's massive apartment and made to trumpet and bellow, but still Kumbhakarn carried on sleeping. It was not until the animals were driven over his great body that he stirred and asked in a drowsy voice, 'Why am I being wakened before the appointed time?'

The demons hastily explained why they had been forced to rouse him, and the giant muttered, 'Ravana has been foolish to anger Rama and these Vanars. Still, to please my brother, I will march against them.'

So, after he had refreshed himself with great quantities of food and wine, Kumbhakarn stumbled out to battle.

The appearance of this terrible giant caused quite a panic amongst the Vanars, thousands of whom were killed as he went crashing through their ranks. But Rama advanced fearlessly with the magic bow which the old sage Agastya had given him. And, to the joy of his followers, he sent an arrow right through the heart of Kumbhakarn.

The giant fell to earth, crushing countless demons beneath his dead body. But now Rama's greatest trial was to come.

Ravana hastily armed himself with all the deadly weapons at his command and rushed upon the prince with howls of rage and defiance. Rama managed to withstand the poisoned darts and spears of his enemy, but it seemed as if his own magic weapons had lost their power. He aimed arrow after arrow at Ravana, yet the demon king remained unharmed.

But at last, just as his strength was beginning to fail him, victory came to Rama.

One arrow, swifter and more powerful than the others, found its way to Ravana's heart. The demon king fell from his chariot and lay dead on the battlefield.

With the death of their king, the hostility of the demons vanished. Laying down their arms, they surrendered to the Vanars. Meanwhile, the prince had entered the city in search of his wife.

Sita was alone in her pavilion, for her terrified guards had long since fled the city. When she heard the sound of footsteps, she looked up in fear lest Ravana had returned, but catching sight of Rama, she rushed forward and fell into his arms with tears of joy.

At first, Rama and Sita could hardly believe that their long separation was at an end, but the happy thought came to the prince that his beloved wife had been found at the very moment when his sentence of banishment was over.

When good Hanuman heard this, he rushed off to Ayodhya to inform Prince Bharat that Rama and Sita were about to return to the kingdom. And the defeated demons brought out a wonderful chariot which they presented to the prince and princess.

Hanuman to the Rescue

Then Rama and Sita stepped into the flower-covered car drawn by swans, and took leave of Lanka forever. The swans flew through the air with the flower-chariot, and brought them swiftly to Ayodhya, where they found the people rejoicing at their return.

Prince Bharat was delighted to hand over the rule of the kingdom to his brother, and the

coronation of Rama and Sita took place at last. There was no jealous soul to spoil the ceremony this time, for Manthara was dead, and Queen Kaikeyi, sorry for what she had done, had asked for and received Rama's forgiveness.

Lakshman received many honours, and good Hanuman returned to his mountain home with gifts for himself and King Sugriv. But what Hanuman valued far more than gold and jewels was the love and gratitude which Rama and Sita and their people would always feel towards him.

Classic Ruskin Bond

*Find more favourite stories for young readers
with brand new illustrations!*

~ANGRY RIVER~

*The Extraordinary Adventure of a Girl Facing
the Fury of an Angry River*
Illustrations by Archana Sreenivasan

How will Sita survive when an angry river sweeps her away? Find out in this classic story of courage and friendship, now in a brand new look.

~ THE BLUE UMBRELLA ~

Illustrations by Archana Sreenivasan

A bittersweet story of a girl, a village and a beautiful silk umbrella, *The Blue Umbrella* is a heart-warmingly funny story that has also been made into an acclaimed film.

~ STORIES SHORT AND SWEET ~

Classic Stories for Children by a Master Storyteller
Illustrations by Archana Sreenivasan

Humour, love, friendship, trust—every emotion, every mood that makes growing up special and worth remembering comes to life in this beautifully illustrated collection.